EMILY AT SCHOOL

Suzanne Williams

Illustrated by Abby Carter

Hyperion Books for Children
New York

For Emily
— S. W.

For Samantha and Carter
—A. C.

With thanks to the estate of Arnold Lobel

Text © 1996 by Suzanne Williams.
Illustrations © 1996 by Abby Carter.

For information address Hyperion Books for Children, 114 Fifth Avenue, New York, New York 10011-5690.
Printed in the United States of America.

First edition
1 3 5 7 9 10 8 6 4 2

The artwork for each picture is prepared using watercolor and pencil.
This book is set in 19-point Goudy.

Library of Congress Cataloging-in-Publication Data
Williams, Suzanne.
    Emily at school / Suzanne Williams ; illustrated by Abby Carter—
    1st ed.
        p.   cm.
    Summary: Emily learns some of the good and bad things about being in second grade.
    ISBN 0-7868-0149-2 (trade)—ISBN 0-7868-1133-1 (pbk.)
    [1. Schools—Fiction. 2. Friendship—Fiction.] I. Carter, Abby, ill. II. Title.
PZ7.W66824Em   1996
[E]—dc20
                                                        96-11174

CONTENTS

Other books by Suzanne Williams

Edwin and Emily

EMILY
AT
SCHOOL

Chapter 1

Second Grade

Emily hopped up and down as she stood in line outside her new classroom. MRS. BROWN. SECOND GRADE said the poster in the window.

"Mrs. Brown in brown letters," Emily said to herself.

At last the classroom door opened. "Welcome to second grade," Mrs. Brown said as the children filed in.

"Thank you," Emily said. She skipped into the room and sat down at one of the desks.

"Can't you read?" said a boy in a striped T-shirt. He pointed to a name tag on the desk. "Alex," he said. "That's me. I'm new, and you are sitting in my chair."

Emily frowned. "I *know* how to read," she said. "I just didn't look at the name tag."

Emily found her desk. It was right in front of Alex's desk and next to Jenny's desk.

Last year she and Jenny had been in the same class. Emily smiled at Jenny. Then she looked back at Alex and stuck out her tongue.

When it was recess time, Emily
put on her jacket and went
outside. She looked around. Alex
was right behind her. Was he
following her? Emily walked fast.

Jenny was waiting for her on
the playground. "Want to play

hopscotch?" Jenny asked.

"Sure," said Emily.

"You go first," Jenny said.

Emily took her hopscotch

chain out of her pocket. She

threw it into the first square.
Then she hopped.

Alex stood watching.

"That new boy in our class is
looking at us," Jenny said.

"I know," said Emily. "His
name is Alex. I think he is
spying on me."

When the bell rang, everyone
ran. So did Emily and Jenny.

"Hey, wait up!" Alex shouted.

"Run harder!" Emily yelled.
"Alex is following us."

Emily and Jenny ran faster.
When they reached the class-

room Emily said, "*Whew!* We made it."

Mrs. Brown opened the door and everyone rushed inside. After all the children had a drink of water, Mrs. Brown

pointed to a bookshelf at the
back of the room. "When your
row is called, you may each
choose a book," she said. "Then
you may find a place to read with

one or two friends."

Emily and Jenny smiled at each other. When it was her turn to choose, Emily picked *Small Pig*, a book she'd read last year.

On her way back, Emily passed Alex's desk. He looked up from his book. "What are *you* reading?" he asked.

Emily showed him.

"I like harder books," Alex said. His book had a lot of words and no pictures.

Emily frowned. "I can read harder books, too," she said. "But

I *like* this one. It has good
pictures and it's really funny."

Jenny came up. "Let's read at
my desk," she said to Emily.

They took turns reading Emily's book first. Emily read one page out loud, then Jenny read the next.

When they finished reading the part where the pig runs away from home, Emily heard someone laugh. She and Jenny looked up. Alex was standing behind them!

"What are you doing?" Jenny asked.

Alex shrugged. "Nothing." He went back to his desk. But instead of reading, Alex put his

head down on top of his book
and closed his eyes.

Poor Alex, thought Emily. He
didn't have anybody to read
with. Maybe he wished he was

still at his old school!

Emily and Jenny looked at each other and then at Alex.

"Should we ask him?" Emily whispered.

Jenny nodded.

Emily got up and went to Alex's desk. "Do you want to read with Jenny and me?" she asked.

Alex opened his eyes and sat up. "Okay," he said.

They finished reading Emily's

book. And when they reached
the part where the pig got stuck
in cement, Alex laughed harder
than anyone else.

14

Chapter 2

Check Marks and Stars

"Sixteen minus seven," Emily read. That was easy! She'd learned to add and subtract *last* year. Emily drew a fat black nine

on her work sheet. She hoped
they would start doing harder
problems soon. She *loved* math.
And she especially liked the stars
Mrs. Brown drew on her papers.

Mrs. Brown handed back
yesterday's work sheets. Emily
stared at hers. At the top of her

paper, where a star should have been, there was a big red –3.

Emily frowned. She always got stars on her papers. Mrs. Brown must have made a mistake.

Emily peeked at Jenny's work sheet. Yes, there was a star on it. She turned around in her seat. Alex's work sheet had a star on it, too. So where was *her* star?

"If there are mistakes on your work sheet," Mrs. Brown told the class, "please correct them. Then put your corrected work sheets in the box on my desk."

Emily stared at her work sheet
again. Then she hunted through
her desk until she found her red
crayon. It would have to do. She
didn't have a red pen.

Carefully, Emily corrected Mrs.
Brown's mistake. She added a

line to the *minus* at the top of her paper and changed it into a *plus*. Then Emily drew a star. It was a bit crooked but it looked okay.

She showed it to Alex. "How do you like my star?" she asked him.

Alex's eyes grew wide. "You shouldn't have done that! Drawing stars is Mrs. Brown's job. She'll be mad."

"But Mrs. Brown made a mistake," Emily said. "She forgot to draw one on my work sheet."

"Oh," said Alex. "Then I guess it's okay."

Emily took her work sheet to Mrs. Brown's desk and put it into the math box. Then she finished her new work sheet.

Emily was cleaning the top of

her desk when the recess bell rang.

"See you on the playground!" Jenny yelled to her and ran out the door with all the other children.

Emily rinsed out her sponge.

Mrs. Brown looked up from her desk, where she sat grading papers. "Emily," she said. "Would you please come here?"

"Yes, Mrs. Brown," Emily said. She wondered if her teacher would give her a special treat for

cleaning her desk so well.

But instead Mrs. Brown held up Emily's math paper. She pointed to the star and the +3. "Did you draw these?" she asked.

"Yes," Emily said. But something was wrong. Mrs.

Brown wasn't smiling.

"*I* am the only one who gives stars in this class," her teacher said.

Emily's face grew warm. Alex was right. Mrs. Brown didn't like anyone to do her job.

Mrs. Brown pointed to three check marks on Emily's work sheet. "The answers to these problems are not right," she said. "But I'm sure you can fix them. Then you may go to recess."

Emily took the work sheet to her desk. She looked at the

problem by the first check mark.

9 + 8 = 16.

Her teacher hadn't made a mistake. *She* had! The other two answers were wrong, too.

Emily's stomach felt funny. She wished she had checked her paper more carefully the first time.

Emily left her corrected paper on Mrs. Brown's desk and went outside. She didn't feel like playing. Mrs. Brown was mad at her. Mrs. Brown didn't like her. She hadn't even noticed Emily's clean desk.

When the bell rang to go back to class, Jenny shouted, "Run, Emily. You'll be late!"

But Emily didn't run. She

wasn't even sure she *liked* second grade anymore.

When she came into the room, Jenny ran up to her. "Come look at your desk!" Jenny said.

Emily looked. Someone had taped a big sheet of paper to the top of her desk. On the paper was a huge star.

SUPER CLEAN DESK said the words under the star. They were brown words. *Mrs.* Brown words.

Emily smiled.

If her teacher wanted to give all the stars, it was all right with her.

When Mrs. Brown gave stars, she really gave stars!

Chapter 3

Emily's Magic Ring

Emily had a new hopscotch chain. It was shinier than her old one. She couldn't wait to try it out. When the recess bell rang, she raced out the door.

"Meet me on the playground," she called back to Jenny.

But when Jenny came, Alex was with her.

"*R-r-r-o-w-l!*" Alex roared. "I'm a monster!"

Emily ignored him. "Let's play
hopscotch," she said to Jenny.

But before Jenny could reply,
Alex roared again. He chased
Jenny over to the jungle gym.
"Into my cave!" he shouted.

Jenny giggled. She climbed inside the bars. "I'm stuck in the monster's cave!" she cried.

"No you're not!" Emily yelled. "Just climb out. Then we can play hopscotch."

"She can't get out!" Alex shouted. "I put a force field around the cave."

"Help!" Jenny cried. "Save me, Emily!"

Emily ran over to the jungle gym. She tried to pull Jenny out.

"The force field," Jenny cried.
"It's too strong!"

Emily frowned. "You're not
even trying to get out."

Alex grabbed Emily's arm.
"Now you're caught, too!" he

shouted. "Get into my cave!"

Emily pulled away. "Stop it!" she yelled. "I want to play hopscotch."

"We *always* play hopscotch," Jenny said. "I want to play this game for a change."

"Well, I don't!" Emily yelled, and she stomped off to the hopscotch court all alone.

Jenny didn't call her to come back and Alex didn't come after her and roar.

Emily took out her new chain. She threw it into the first square. Slowly, Emily began to hop. When

she got to the middle, she
stopped. Playing hopscotch by
herself wasn't much fun.

Emily picked up her chain.

She twisted it around her finger. Now her chain looked like a ring. A *magic* ring.

Emily ran back to the jungle gym.

"*R-r-r-o-w-l!*" roared Alex.

"My magic ring will turn you into a frog," Emily told him. She pointed her ring at Alex. "*Zap!*" she shouted.

Alex hopped up and down. "*Ribbit. Ribbit,*" he croaked.

Emily giggled. So did Jenny.

"Now I will break the force

field," Emily said. She pointed
her ring at the cave.

"*Zap!*" she shouted. The force
field crumbled. Emily pulled

Jenny out of the bars just as the
bell rang.

Emily and Jenny and Alex
started back to class.

"We can play hopscotch at the

next recess," Jenny said. "Okay,
Emily?"

"*Ribbit*," croaked Alex.

Emily grinned. "Let's *all* be frogs," she said. "Frogs are very good at *hop*scotch."